SUPER Survival Senses

Dear Reader

Humans and animals use their senses to interact with the world around them. Their senses help them to survive in all kinds of environments – in the air, on land and in the sea.

> “SOME ANIMALS HAVE SENSES THAT HUMANS LACK, FOR EXAMPLE BEES, BIRDS AND SOME FISH CAN DETECT MAGNETIC FIELDS AND PLATYPUS CAN DETECT ELECTRICITY.”

I've found out about some amazing animals that use their senses in remarkable ways, in order to survive.

I hope you enjoy reading about them as much as I enjoyed writing about them for this book.

Sharon Parsons

NELSON
CENGAGE Learning™
For learning solutions, visit **cengage.com.au**

Contents

SUPER Survival Senses

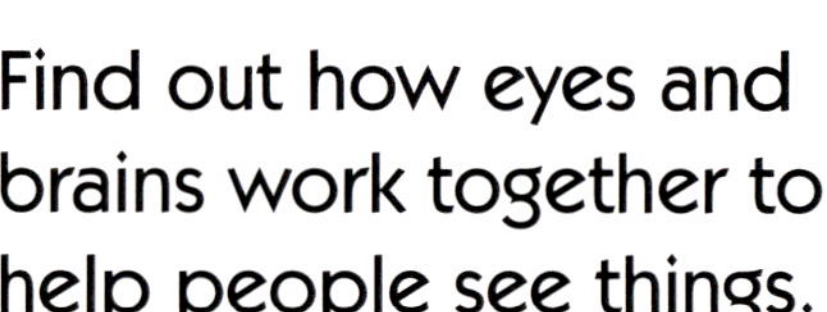

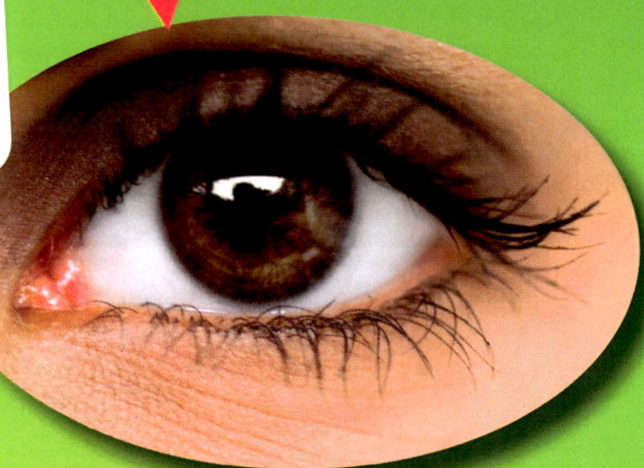

1 How Many Senses Do We Have?

Make **Sense** of Senses

Humans have five main senses: sight, smell, hearing, taste and touch. The five sense organs are the eyes, nose, ears, tongue and skin.

Nerves send messages from the sense organs along the spinal cord to the brain. It is the brain and the spinal cord that make sense of our senses!

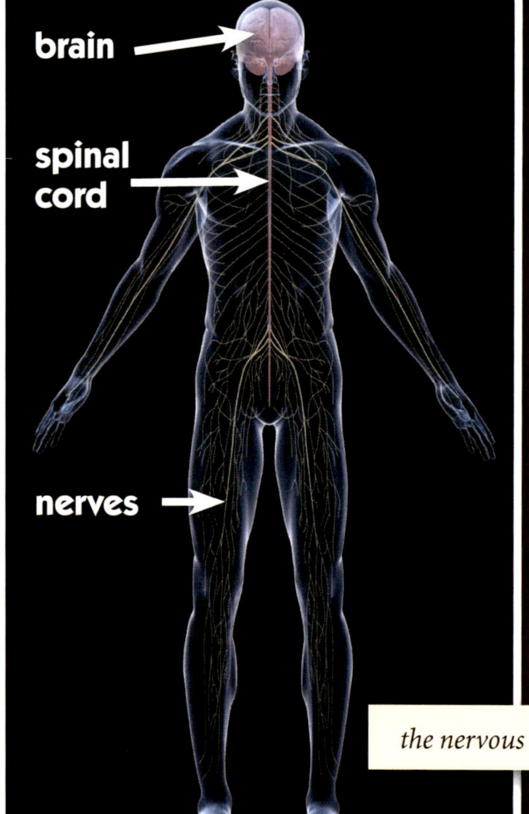

the nervous system

Sense of Sight

The eyes detect, or sense, light bouncing off the things we see. Nerves carry information from the eyes to the brain, which makes sense of what we see.

Sense of Smell

A smell is like a cloud of tiny scent particles floating in the air. The nose detects, or senses, these particles. Nerves carry information from the nose to the brain, which makes sense of what we smell.

Sense of Hearing

The ears detect vibrations in the air from things we hear. Nerves carry information from the ears to the brain, which makes sense of what we hear.

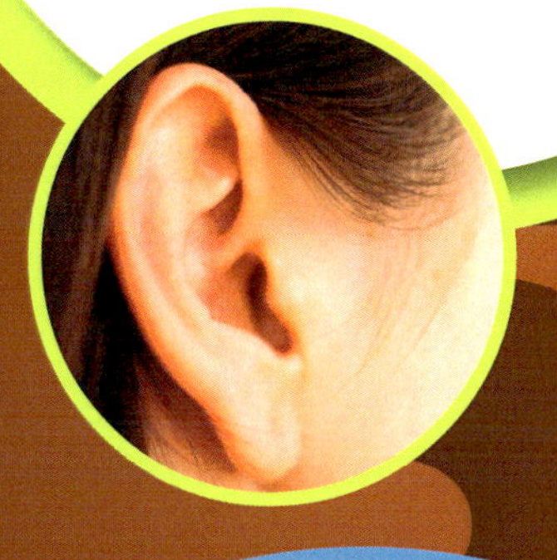

Sense of Taste

The tongue and mouth detect tiny particles that are sweet, sour, salty, bitter or savoury. Nerves carry information from the tongue to the brain, which decides whether something tastes good or bad. Our sense of smell also affects what we taste.

Sense of Touch

Different nerves in the skin detect when the body is in pain, or being touched. Nerves carry information to the brain, which makes sense of what we feel.

Are There More Senses?

The body has other senses, too. One of those senses is called thermoception. It is the sense that senses temperature.

2 How Eyes Work

Eyes Protect You

Eyes are like "windows to the world".

Light bounces off objects and enters the eyes. Light triggers nerves to send messages to the brain. The brain then decodes these messages into a picture inside the brain.

For example, if we look at a car speeding towards us, the brain "warns" us in a flash. This process happens very quickly, so a person can see what is in front of them instantly.

Understanding the sense of sight helps to explain why it is important for everyone to look after their eyes.

Life Science

Why Do We Blink?

People blink about once every six seconds. This helps keep the eye moist. Blinking also stops irritating particles from entering the eyes.

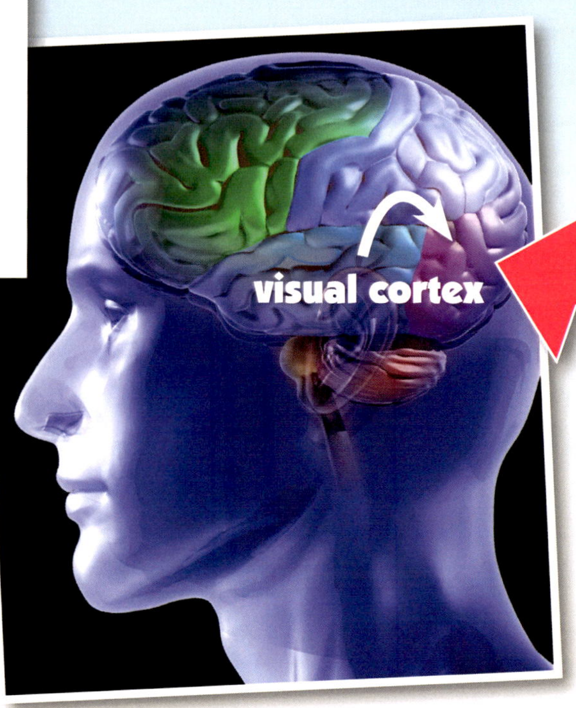

1

When an eye is open, light comes in through the eye's **cornea** and then goes through the **pupil** and the **lens**.

2

The light then hits the **retina**, an area at the back of the eye that is sensitive to light and colour.

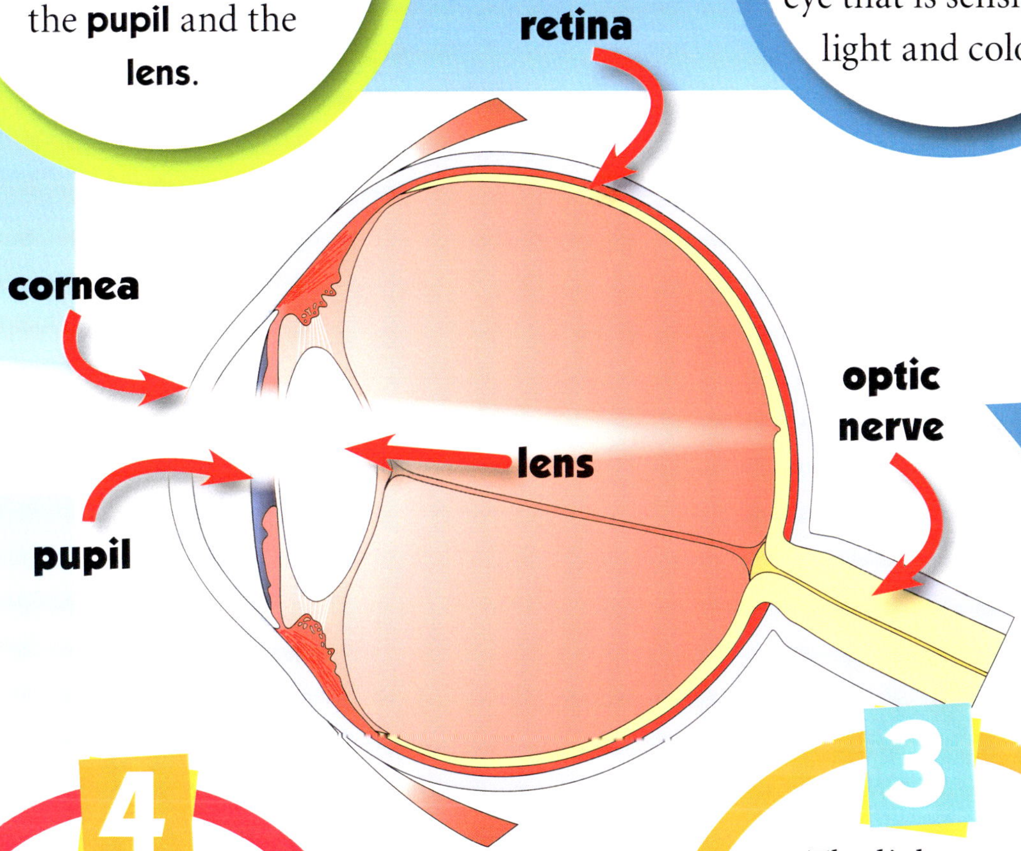

retina

cornea

optic nerve

lens

pupil

3

The light stops at the retina. Behind the retina, electrical messages are sent along the **optic nerve** to a part of the brain called the **visual cortex**.

4

The **visual cortex** takes these messages and builds a "picture" of what the eyes are sensing, instantly!

HEALTH FEATURE
Protect Your Eyes

Simple ways to protect your eyes are described below.

The Sun: Never look directly at the Sun, even for a moment.

Sunglasses: Wear sunglasses that block out the Sun's ultraviolet-A and ultraviolet-B rays.

Bright lights: Use good light when you're reading, writing or working on the computer. This stops your eyes from getting tired.

Sharp objects: Walk, don't run, when holding sharp objects, such as scissors, pens, pencils and rulers. Hold them down and away from your body.

Keep your eyes protected from the Sun with sunglasses.

OPTICS AND OPTICAL

Optics: the study of light and the way it behaves.

Optical: anything to do with light.

An optometrist tests a boy's eyesight.

Eye Care

Eyes at school: Can you clearly see the words in your books and at the front of the classroom? If not, tell your parents, teacher or school nurse. You may need to visit an optometrist.

Eyes in sports: Wear eye guards when playing games like baseball and cricket to avoid injury. You could wear goggles when swimming in pools.

OPTOMETRISTS AND OPHTHALMOLOGISTS

Optometrist: someone who tests people's eyes. The tests show if the person's eyes are healthy or if glasses or contact lenses are needed.

Ophthalmologist: an eye doctor.

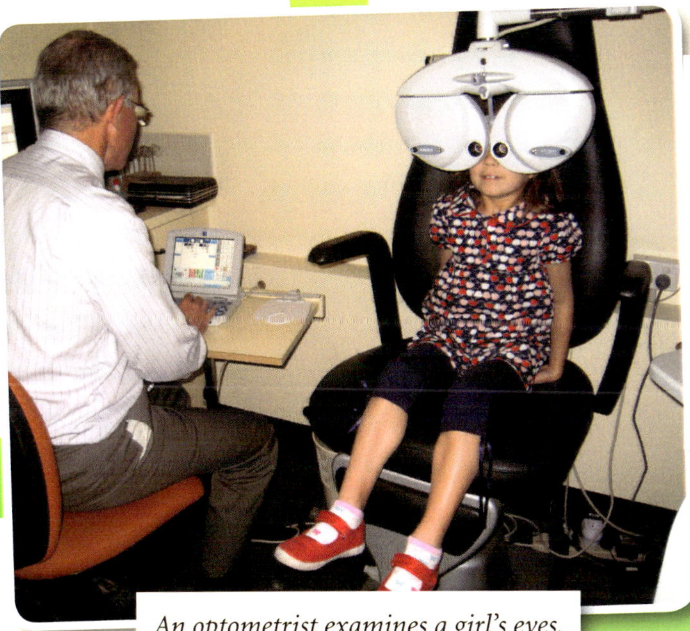

An optometrist examines a girl's eyes.

Life Science

Eye Muscles

The eyes are surrounded by muscles that move them up, down and sideways. The brain controls the eye muscles.

a medical model of the eye

Amazing Animal Survival Senses

Animal Senses From Underground and Up

Animals have senses just like humans do. But some animals do not have or need all five senses. They use what senses they have to survive in different environments.

Using Survival Senses in the Dark

Bats use echolocation to help them fly and locate things in the dark. Echoes bounce off flying insects. The bats then locate the insects, and catch and eat them. Echoes also bounce off cave walls and other bats, so the bats do not crash!

a bat in flight

ECHOLOCATION

When a bat squeaks, the sound is so high-pitched that humans cannot hear it. But the bat can. It can also tell if the sound is bouncing back or echoing off something nearby.

Life Science

An Iguana's Sense of Touch

The iguana can sense when sand is the right temperature for laying its eggs.

Is the sand the right temperature?

Using Survival Senses UNDER the Ground

Animals that live underground often do not use their sense of sight. They use other senses to live and escape from predators, such as ants and earthworms.

Ants: Ants have eyes but they use their sense of smell more. They use their antennae to smell, taste and touch.

Ants also use sound vibrations. If an ant gets trapped in an ant tunnel, it makes a loud sound vibration to alert other ants to come and free it.

an ant close-up

Earthworms:
Earthworms do not have eyes, but have cells that sense light. And their whole body is covered with taste sensors!

When earthworms sense movement in the soil, they try to escape quickly in case a predator is after them.

an earthworm

Skunks: Skunks can live almost anywhere – underground in burrows, as well as above the ground. Skunks are clever because they use the other animal's sense of smell to defend themselves.

When a predator comes close to attack, the skunk sprays an awful-smelling liquid. The predator would rather run away than eat something that smells that bad.

A skunk relies on smell.

Elephants have good hearing.

Elephants: Large ears give elephants an excellent sense of hearing. They can hear very low sounds, which people cannot hear.

a chameleon is watching

Chameleons: Imagine being able to revolve each eye separately in many directions. That's what a chameleon can do! It uses its revolving eyes and good sense of sight to spot predators. It would be very difficult to sneak up on a chameleon.

A chameleon can change its colours to blend into its surroundings. It also has a great sense of touch and taste. Sometimes its tongue can be longer than its whole body!

Pit Vipers: A pit viper's tongue has no tastebuds. Its tongue darts out and bring smells into its mouth where it senses them.

A pit viper also has pits, or pores, between its eyes and nostrils that sense the temperature of prey. For example, it can sense the temperature of a mouse from up to 40 centimetres away.

Using Survival Senses UNDER the Sea

Dolphins: These mammals use echolocation to detect food and predators – usually sharks. They make clicks with their mouths, then listen for the sound that bounces off whatever is nearby.

Their hearing is excellent, and they can taste, but not smell.

Life Science

A Four-Eyed Fish

A species of fish called Anableps have eyes divided in half, so they can see in the air and the water at the same time. They spend most of their time on the surface of the water.

a four-eyed fish

Octopuses: Octopuses have very good senses, especially touch, sight and taste. They can taste with their tentacles!

Octopuses are very intelligent. If some food is placed inside a bottle, octopuses are clever enough to work out how to unscrew the bottle top with their tentacles. Octopuses have nerve centres like mini-brains in each one of their eight tentacles.

An octopus can unscrew a bottle top to get to the food inside.

an octopus

Using Survival Senses BELOW and ON the Ice

Penguins: These birds have a very good sense of sight underwater. Penguins have flat corneas, which act like a pair of glasses to help them see more clearly underwater.

Having a good sense of sight helps penguins to catch fish and spot predators.

Adélie penguins and leopard seals resting on ice floes in Antarctica

a polar bear

a Weddell seal

Polar Bears: Polar bears have an excellent sense of smell. They can smell a seal hiding under one-metre thick ice! Their noses detect animal scents on air currents.

Seals: Seal senses include touch, smell, taste, sight and hearing. Their sense of small is not very developed, but their hearing and vision are excellent.

Scientists think some seals may also use echolocation, because they make clicks underwater, like dolphins.

Using Survival Senses IN the Air

Moths: Moths use their sense of smell to find other moths. Female moths put out a faint smell that male moths can detect. When they meet, they mate and the female then lays eggs.

tiger moths mating

an emperor gum moth

Life Science

Thousands of Eye Lenses

Dragonflies have thousands of lenses in each of their five eyes. In one eye alone, they could have 30 000 lenses!

a dragonfly

a golden eagle

Eagles: Eagles have an excellent sense of sight. While soaring high in the air, eagles can spot their prey far below.

Their eyeballs are large – about 35 millimetres in diameter. Human eyeballs are only 24 millimetres in diameter. An eagle's eyesight is two to three times better than a human's.

Falcons: Falcons have similar eyesight to eagles. In the air, falcons can see a 10-centimetre-long object from a distance of 1.5 kilometres!

a falcon sitting on a perch

Life Science

Tasting With Feet!

Butterflies and blowflies have taste receptors on their feet.

Bees have taste receptors on their front legs, jaws, and antennae.

a butterfly

4 Zebras' Survival Senses

There's **More** to a **Zebra** than its Stripes

A zebra's senses, stripes and speed help it to survive against predators in Africa. Their main predators are lions, leopards and cheetahs. Lions often try to attack zebras at night and at dawn, so zebras are always on guard. All their senses are on alert!

Zebra Senses and Speed

Zebras have excellent senses of sight, smell, hearing and taste. If they sense a predator trying to sneak up on a zebra foal, the herd will quickly move into a circle around the foal to protect it.

a herd of zebras escaping from a cheetah

Zebras Sense All Around

Zebras have eyes on the sides of their heads, so they can see in most directions. They also have good night vision. Zebras can turn their large ears in the direction of any sound to hear more clearly.

Stripes Help Survival

Zebra stripes help them to survive in the wild. The speedy "blur" of their stripes can confuse predators when the zebras gallop at great speed across the plains.

5 The Mosquito's Super Sense of Smell

A Mosquito's Need for Blood

Everyone has probably had a mosquito sucking on them at one time or other – especially in summer. But mosquitoes do not actually eat our blood. They get their food source from sugar in plant liquids, such as nectar and juice.

It's the female mosquitoes that need blood – to develop their eggs. So all mosquito bites come from the females!

A Mosquito's Sense of Smell

Mosquitoes are attracted to humans because of their smell. Mosquitoes like body odour – especially foot odour.

Mosquitoes use their sense of smell to find a human, then they use their sense of touch. They like warm, sweaty bodies.

Malaria Mosquitoes

Not every mosquito is a malaria mosquito. The kind that carries malaria is the *Anopheles* mosquito. It is found mostly in Africa, Asia and South America. Malaria mosquitoes kill around one million people per year by spreading the virus – they are more deadly than any other animal.

a mosquito on human skin

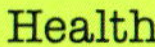

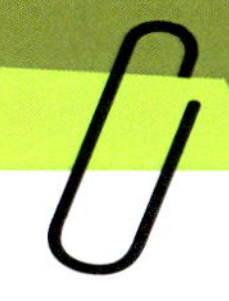

"I'm glad they're not really THAT big!"

What Is Malaria?

Malaria is a disease caused by parasites. A mosquito may suck up some tiny malaria parasites when it bites a person with malaria. When it bites someone else, it injects some parasites mixed with its saliva into that person, who then becomes infected with the deadly disease.

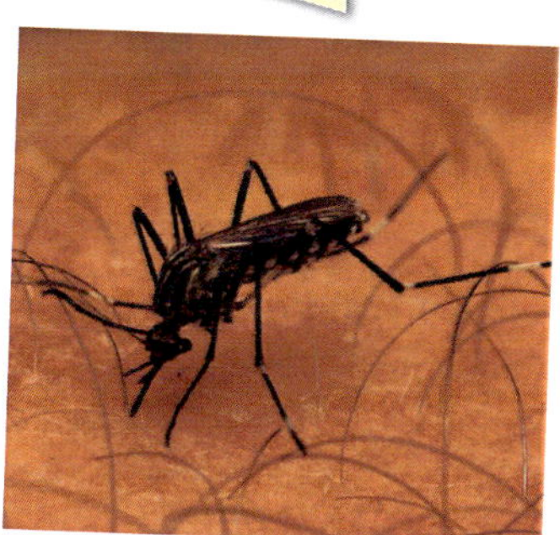

a mosquito biting a person's arm

Malaria Research

Many scientists research malaria to try to help treat the huge number of people who suffer and die from malaria every year. For example, scientists in Norway who work for the World Health Organisation (WHO) study the human body smells that malaria mosquitoes are attracted to.

Scientists want to find a good insect repellent against malaria mosquitoes for people to put on their skin. They want a repellent that will smell so awful to mosquitoes that they will buzz off!

The trick is to find a smell that only mosquitoes, and not people, dislike. We need to trick their senses, not our own.

Index

Glossary

air currents	Streams of air in the atmosphere that move in a certain direction
nerves	Cells that are used to send signals to and from the brain from our organs, muscles and skin
nervous system	The group of nerves and other cells that is controlled by the brain
parasites	Organisms that feed off, or live within, another living thing
predator	An animal that feeds itself by hunting and eating other animals
receptors	Cells that can sense changes in the environment, such as heat, smell or taste
spinal cord	A central bundle of nerves that runs up an animal's spine (if it has one)
ultra-violet A and B	Ultra-violet A and B are two different shades of invisible light given off by the Sun. Too much ultra-violet B can cause sunburn.